I bought a doctor's book from Eatons
It was down at Regina then.
It cost me three dollars, yes.

But I read that book from end to end.
I learned it by heart.
At night in my kitchen by candlelight.

It was this thick and it had pictures
About everything—mother, baby, boils, breaks,
Yes, I learned it by heart.

I said, "I'm not scared to help them."
No doctors, nobody; so I learned that book
And I helped them.

This vignette of a passing way of life is an introduction to the words of
Mary Augusta Tappage. Born in February 1899 in British Columbia's
Cariboo country, she was the granddaughter of a Shuswap chief. When
Augusta was in her eighties, she shared with Jean Speare the memories of a
lifetime lived in harmony with the land and in fidelity to her heritage. This
book had its beginnings in those conversations.

THE DAYS OF
AUGUSTA

THE DAYS OF AUGUSTA

EDITED BY JEAN E. SPEARE

PHOTOGRAPHY BY ROBERT KEZIERE

Douglas & McIntyre
Vancouver/Toronto

92 93 94 95 96   5 4 3 2 1

Douglas & McIntyre, 1615 Venables Street, Vancouver, BC
V5L 2H1

Canadian Cataloguing in Publication Data

Evans, Augusta, 1888 – 1978
      The days of Augusta
      ISBN 1-55054-003-3
      1. Evans, Augusta, 1888 – 1978.   2. Shuswap Indians—
Biography.   3. Indians of North America—British Columbia—
Biography.   I. Speare, Jean E., 1921 –   II. Title
FC3817.3.E92 1992   971.1′004979   C92-091052-1
F1087.E92 1992

Cover design by Barbara Hodgson
Book design by Sally Bryer
Typesetting by Vancouver Typesetting Co. Ltd.
Printed in Canada by D. W. Friesen & Sons Ltd.
Printed on acid-free paper

Contents

Preface

Augusta, christened "Mary Augusta Tappage," was born at Soda Creek in the Cariboo country of British Columbia on February 11, 1888. She was the daughter of Mary Ann Longshem and Christopher (Alex) Tappage.

Her paternal grandfather was partly French, one of many who came west from the prairie following the arrest of Louis Riel. He spoke often of the Red River Valley, and she believed this to have been his birthplace. He spoke French fluently.

Her maternal grandfather was locally born William Longshem (as near as she could give spelling to the name), chief of the Soda Creek Indians. His wife, "Ginny," taught Augusta the crafts necessary to an Indian living on the high plateau lands.

At the age of four she was taken away to school at St. Joseph's Mission, a large Catholic mission in the Onward Valley near Williams Lake. Augusta spoke in many different moods of her life at the Mission School: from elation to frustration.

"What I could never understand, we weren't allowed to speak our language. If we were heard speaking Shuswap, we were punished. We were made to write on the board one hundred times, 'I will not speak Indian any more.'" Augusta shrugged and gave a little laugh. "And now we are supposed to remember our language and our skills because they are almost lost. Well, they're going to be hard to get back because the new generations are not that interested."

"I wasn't happy at home after I got out of school," said Augusta. "Everything was different. I could see things happening to my people that I didn't like, but what could I do? I was still too young."

In Augusta's childhood, the Cariboo was a land still trembling from the onslaught of goldseekers with their picks and shovels. The sod was being turned for the first time by settlers from faraway places, and the rangelands of the Chilcotin were becoming dotted with herds of beef cattle. It was a time of hopeful, yet painful, pioneering for those who adopted the Cariboo as their home; perhaps even more for the native people, who faced bewildering changes because of the intruders.

Augusta remembered most vividly the changes which brought about the influx of people: the canoes yielding to steamboats, for Soda Creek was the southern terminus for upper Fraser navigation; the Indian trails that first laced the country being followed by the Cariboo wagon road with its oxen and pack trains, its freight teams and stage coaches. And then she saw the paved highway, the railway and the airplanes.

If Augusta ever resisted these changes, it was with a fraction of the energy she gave to each day's living, for she lived every day to the full extent of her physical and mental strength.

Discharged from the Mission at thirteen, Augusta spent the next two years under the tutelage of her beloved grandmother. "George Evans came along and it wasn't long before I got married. December, 1903, sometime between Christmas and the New Year. Father Thomas married us in the little church down on the reservation."

Through her marriage to the son of a Welshman, Augusta became non-status, although George's mother was a Shuswap of the Sugar Cane reserve.

Augusta and her husband lived at first with her parents while George worked at one of the large ranches in the vicinity. Then they decided to get their own farm. They pre-empted one hundred and sixty-six acres on the banks of Deep Creek, not far from Augusta's birthplace.

"We had three years to pay off the farm and we did — but it was hard work. One way we were lucky. In those days you could work off your taxes by doing work on the road, so that's what George did."

Their family began to arrive: first a boy, then a daughter who died at birth; then another son, and a second daughter who also died at birth.

"And my two boys, Joseph and George, they never went to school. Taxpayers' children couldn't go to the Mission. Well, I didn't care about that. But there was no other school close by, so I taught them myself. Yes, I guess they can read and reckon as good as most folk can. I taught them myself."

Together, Augusta and George fished and hunted. They planted a garden. They had chickens and, using a preservative salve to coat the eggs, they stored these away for the winter along with dairy foods, bottled fruits and vegetables.

"I made my own soap — many women made their own soap. And we always had good crops of wheat. After it was threshed, we took it to the grist mill on Deep Creek and had it made into flour. We got oats crushed for animal and chicken feed. Later there was another flour mill. There were several all through the country. They helped to bring down the high cost of flour. It was expensive when it had to be freighted in."

Shopping, in the teen years of the century, meant going into Soda Creek. There were two general stores at that time. One was owned by Robert McLeese, after whom McLeese Lake was named. The other was Dunlevey's — run by Peter Curran Dunlevey, a man famous in the Cariboo for having made the first gold strike on the Horsefly River in 1859.

At these two stores they could buy dried fruits, split peas, beans, rice, barley, sugar and sago, all sold by the pound out of 100-pound gunny sacks. They could buy yard goods, but few ready-made clothes.

"I made all our clothes. I sewed them by hand. Dresses were easy, but men's shirts and pants, they were hard! Two women good with needle and thread could make a man's shirt in a day.

"Later when we could afford it, George got me a sewing machine. We paid $19.00 for it from Simpsons in Winnipeg. It took quite a while to get here; after it got to Ashcroft by train it had to come to Soda Creek by freight team. But I was sure glad to see it. It just came to the freight shed. There was no post office in those days."

Augusta was still a young woman when her husband died. He had been ill for a long time; an operation in Vancouver was too late, and he continued to live in failing health for three years after it. Augusta buried him in the graveyard at St. Joseph's Mission.

Not long after, she buried her elder son, Joseph, beside his father, and went to live on Joseph's farm, from where she could look down over the river benches to the Soda Creek Reserve. The farm at Deep Creek was taken over by the second son, George.

"I didn't have much heart for it after he was gone."

She took work in various homes in the district, cooking and cleaning. Unfortunate children needing a home and loving care found both beneath her roof until they were old enough to move on. It did not seem unusual that she never had the chance to travel beyond the hills of Cariboo.

Grandchildren arrived and great-grandchildren. Augusta went on teaching them all. Although the young were not as receptive as she once was to learning the old ways, her grandchildren did learn to converse with her in their own language as well as English. Shuswap is not a written language and can be fostered only through speech. Augusta used every opportunity to keep it alive and actually won her cause over an age that was moving too fast to listen. She spoke resolutely and her philosophy was obvious:

"Life was good," she said. "I have not been idle altogether."

Augusta Evans died on August 16, 1978, at the age of ninety. She was buried in the native graveyard on the Soda Creek Reserve. Nearby is the grave of her great-grandson, Sammy, to whom one of the poems in her book is dedicated. Sammy predeceased Augusta when he drowned in the Fraser River while netting salmon. Also nearby is the more recent grave of her son, George.

Augusta would be proud of the young natives growing up on her ancient bench-lands, meeting the challenge of a new era with competence and with good spirit— Canada's first people.

The Holdup

My aunt told us. We were excited.

It was at Three-mile Creek
there at the Hundred-and-Fifty-Mile on the old trail;
well the same way you go to Ashcroft now;
well here is this creek,
they call it Three-Mile.

It was all bushy
right to the edge of the trail it was bush;
the government didn't cut right-of-ways
in those days, no —
so it was all bush.

The date I don't know how long ago it was.
I must have been out of school,
married and out of school.
We were in mountain meadows
my husband and I, cutting hay.

When we came back my aunt told us.

Anyhow this place was bushy
and here the robbers must have waited
till the stage went by. "Stop!"
They told the driver to stop
but he was hard-of-hearing.

Many people were on the stage
some inside, some out, riding on top
by the driver, all from Barkerville, yes,
going to Ashcroft from Barkerville —
every week, up and down, up and down.

The driver, he didn't stop, no,
when they told him. They shot at him
above his horses. They didn't kill a soul.
They scared the horses.
I think they scared everyone.

My aunt told us everyone was scared.

But the driver was strong, I guess,
and the man who rode beside him;
together they controlled the horses,
together they made the horses stop
by Three-Mile Creek.

They took the mailbags, the robbers did,
the bags, some has money, some has mail;
I couldn't tell you what all they had,
but they took them
and ransacked them.

They didn't hurt anyone
but they emptied the bags, took the money.
It doesn't say gold; I never heard gold.
But they came from Barkerville
and maybe there was gold.

But my aunt didn't say 'gold'.

There were some of us suspiscious
who they were, yes, we thought local maybe,
but we couldn't tell; we couldn't say
who robbed the stage,
who took the money.

But when we came from making hay, my husband and I,
this is what my aunt told us.

The Sick Woman

This woman — they used to camp down Soda Creek and all the rest left her and went up to that Tyee Lake, yes. That's where they used to catch their fish in the springtime, yes, in the springtime.

Well, this woman was sick with rheumatics. I guess it must have been rheumatics because she lay stiff there and wouldn't move. They had to pack her water there when they left her and I guess some fish — was all they had to eat you know in those days.

They left her there in the tent or some kind of covering and it's where they left her. They never expected her to live. Her relatives went to Tyee Lake. I guess they had to make fish because they have nothing much to eat after the winter. They eat their fish and their dry meat and they couldn't hunt, you know, not like the people of our days.

Well anyway, this old lady she was sick with rheumatics and she was left alone there to die I guess. To die or live, it was either one of the two. Yes.

And in those days nobody knew anything about the sun — how it will cure your bones. How it will cure you if you take sunbaths — in those days nobody believed in that.

But I guess she was laying down all the time out in the sun, all alone, nobody but herself. I guess when she'd get hungry she'd eat the dry fish. I don't know if she had any fire. There was no matches in those days, no. But I guess she used to help herself.

The old folks used to make their fire between two rocks with one of those black flints. They used to turn it like that, yes, between their hands; turn it like that and it would fire. When it fires, it used to burn this dry hay that you find on sidehills. It's been dry and white, yes, it would take the place of paper and that would burn. That was their fire.

You couldn't get them stuck, you know. They had to do something. Yes.

Well anyhow, this old lady, I guess she got tired laying down and she managed to wiggle her toes and move her fingers. Finally she sat up. How many days after they left her, it doesn't say, but she must have sat up, and in the meantime, she could move her feet, up and down like that, wiggle her toes and move her arms. How fast, I couldn't tell you, but she did!

And in the meantime, she managed to stand up. Her stick was her cane, yes. She stood up, but she couldn't walk! She just stood up. I guess she was kind of shaky. So she sat down and laid down and she kept it up until she could walk.

Well, when she could walk, she walked all over that place, Soda Creek, where they left her, you know, to die. Yes, she walked and walked. She was happy to walk again, I guess. Her rheumatics were all gone, yes.

So finally the same day, she thought about Tyee Lake and she said to herself,

"I'm going out there. I'm going to see Tyee Lake and eat some fish."

Well she got up — what lunch she took, it doesn't say, but it must have been fish. So off she went.

And Tyee Lake, you know, is a long way from Soda Creek. I guess she camped somewhere on the trail. But I guess she was quite strong by now and she was determined to go.

Well, the next day or so she made Tyee Lake, the camping ground where it's a kind of side hill and there is the lake right here, see, the lake is right here. And there is the camping place and trees, cottonwoods and trees over there, all over.

Well, she got up and these people were eating their meal. It was their dinner time meal. It couldn't have been the supper time meal and I guess when they saw her, they got scared of her. They thought it was her ghost, yes. Why was she walking? She walked right where they had been eating and they all left in the woods and ran off.

Well, she sat down and she started to eat. I guess she was hungry and she tells them, "Come over here, it's me. Me that you left to die. But I didn't die. It's me. Come on, don't be afraid of me. It's me!"

Well I guess some of the bravest ones came out, the menfolk. Finally they all came out and she told them how she made it. How she used to take sunbaths all the time, all day long. Finally she could wiggle her hands and move her feet, her toes. Finally she said she sat up. She told them and then when she could walk, stood up. She stood up with her stick, but she didn't walk right away.

I guess it took some strength. She wasn't very strong, you know. Well, I guess in the meantime, she made it to walk.

Well, she walked all around that place where they left her. Well when she could walk that much she went to Tyee Lake, yes.

Yes, they didn't seem to care much for her, but she didn't care for anybody either as long as she was alive, you know. And I guess she was kind of sore at them because they had left her to die, but she didn't die.

People long ago wouldn't have bothered with no sick people. No. They leave them to die or live, it was either one of the two.

Tyee — Big Chief

Tyee Lake was called after big chief — it means big chief.
But *Tyee* is not Shuswap.
It's Chinook, I think.
But it's not my language.

Pashish'kwa — that means lake in my language.
Shadad'kwa — that means river.

I can't tell you how to spell it.
But that's how we say it.
It's a hard language, Shuswap — real hard.

When I got out of Mission school
I had to ask what the Indians were saying.
I couldn't understand them.
We were only allowed to speak English at school.
I almost forgot my own language.
It's Shuswap, my language.

The Lillooets

That was a big cloud of dust 'way down
to the south in the spring, yes.
It was the Lillooet Indians coming north,
coming north to the goldfields
up by Barkerville.

They go north into that country to work,
to work all the time, hard,
horses and wagons, women and children,
and dogs, hiyu dogs, all going
up by Barkerville.

They work from the time they get there
till fall, till the leaves drop, yes,
and the snow comes and it freezes
the lakes and the creeks
up by Barkerville.

It was the Lillooets going by in the spring
with packing horses, packing freight, yes,
into the mines somewhere in the mountains
and into the creeks
up by Barkerville.

All from Lillooet and I see them passing,
They are passing and passing and, no,
I couldn't ask them where they go —
they speak a different language,
but they go up by Barkerville.

We speak Shuswap, all of us Shuswap —
Soda Creek, Sugar Cane, Alkali, Canoe Creek,
Dog Creek, Canim Lake — all speak Shuswap,
except the Lillooets who go
up by Barkerville.

They come back in the fall, these Lillooets,
tired, I guess, but lots of money, lots of fish,
not minding snow or mud. They laugh
thinking of summer, yes,
up by Barkerville.

Christmas at the Mission

I remember Christmas at the Mission.
Always we used to have midnight mass.

But we didn't know about Christmas and holidays
Until the Sisters came.
The Sisters came from France, you know,
And they brought Christmas with them.

They were the Sisters of Infant Jesus,
Those who came.

The teachers who had been teaching us before,
They didn't bother or care
Or hold Christmas. When the Sisters came
Was when we first knew Christmas!

The Sisters made us a Christmas concert, taught us
To sing hymns and songs,
Say recitations to everybody, helped us
Decorate our first Christmas tree.

I can't tell you how beautiful that first Christmas tree!
Everything was changed!

And our shoe, our right shoe, had to be polished
And put up on a bench
On Christmas Eve for holding candies, yes,
And whatever present you were going to get.

And then we all went to chapel through the snow
That first Christmas for midnight mass.

At Mission School

Yes, I remember my days at the Mission school. It was fun, once you got used to it.

I was a small girl to start — I can't remember when my mother dumped me there. I know mama was there with me, but when she left, I never saw her.

There were no Sisters at that time. The Sisters of St. Anne must have shut down, closed down, I don't know why. But that's what they were saying.

When I started, there were white women there. You see, the next time they opened the doors, two white women were teaching us — Mrs. Lancaster and Mrs. Richardson. Mrs. Harry Horne was the cook. They were good and kind. I don't know where they came from to tell the truth, but they stayed and stayed for years. Yes, they stayed and stayed.

The Fathers were there too. I guess they got paid, you know; I guess they all got paid.

The old lady was old — Mrs. Richardson was old. Mrs. Lancaster wasn't old; neither was Mrs. Harry Horne. She used to cook for us, cook for everybody. She used to do it all alone. After she left, the bigger girls took the cooking on, yes. Three of them. One cooks, one serves. I guess one helps peel potatoes and sets the tables and everything.

We went to school in the mornings about ten o'clock. The bell would ring. I would go to school. I would stay there till dinner time. Twelve o'clock.

They taught us everything, everything; reading, writing, figuring — not sewing — no, not during school hours. The sewing was from four o'clock till six. We had to patch. We had to patch the boys' clothes. We had to wash and iron Mondays, Tuesdays. We had to patch and keep on patching till Saturday and all their bags would be lined up. They had numbers, see. They had numbers. Each bag had a number. All the clothes that goes into this bag had the same number. Every pupil a number.

It wasn't bad, patching. But we liked to be out instead of staying in the school.

Now as I see it, as I see it now, I didn't learn enough. No I didn't learn enough. Should have looked after my book instead of closing it when it got hot. I'd close the arithmetic. I'd close the grammar book. And I'd turn my face to the wall. And they'd punish me. They'd make me kneel down in a corner with my book — but I'd never open my book. I'd just kneel there and get punished. Oh, my knees used to get sore, but I never looked at my book, No, not till the next day at school.

We all slept in one big room. Bigger than this house, the room. It took all the children, all the grades. Girls in one, boys in another, sleeping rooms.

The children came from all over the reserves, Sugar Cane, Soda Creek, Alkali, Canoe Creek, Dog Creek, Canim Lake, Quesnel, in those days. Yes. They came by stage if their parents couldn't bring them. Horse stage — the stages, yes, were driven by horses. And they'd get down to the Mission with the stage. If their parents couldn't come, the stage would take them home.

There was no one from Chilcotin, no — too far away, out there, far away.

We didn't have vacation for a long time. They didn't give us vacation. We'd stay there all year. Pick berries in the summertime from July to September. Then we'd go back to school. We'd use the berries at the mission in the winter. We'd be there all winter.

Little kids used to be homesick for their homes. Oh, yes, they used to cry at night. They were small, like this. Toward the end we got used to the Mission, we used to play, recreation time, they called it, all run in the yard and play, run and play, do everything.

I didn't see my mother and father much. Sometimes they'd come and see us. Maybe three times a year. Sometimes we'd get lonesome for them, but what could we do? We couldn't do nothing. No phones, there was nothing those days. Messages by mouth is all.

I guess they missed us, after we grew up. But they never missed us while I was small and useless. I know they didn't, I don't just think so!

It was compulsory I guess in those days to go to the Mission school. It's worse now. Compulsory education everywhere now, you know. They put you to jail if you don't put your children to school, and who wants to be put to jail?

But it was nice.

We had little gardens. They had a board fence around and we used to raise flowers, pansies and sweet williams. I like that. We used to have a ditch full of water running down there, and we'd water our gardens till they bloomed. It used to be nice yes, nice to see some flowers in those dry hills — sand and sage — and then some flowers.

But we didn't have many seeds. Just pansies and sweet williams, but no roses. When the sisters came, they had lilacs. Lots of lilacs. We had to dry up the pansy seeds and save them. The Sister used to make us pick them for her and she would dry them for another year.

It was nice there at the Mission school. I liked it but I think now I didn't learn enough. I didn't keep my books open enough!

Thoughts of the Mission School

I

It's different now when Sammy goes to school. We wait on the road for the down bus. This time, last week, the Mission bus came along. No stages and horses these days. That's gone!

It was my intention to take him as far as Williams Lake but when this bus came along, Sammy says, "You don't have to come."

The down bus drops us at Three-Mile Creek and then we walk in from there. Oh, it's quite a walk from Three-Mile Creek to the Mission after we get off the bus you know.

Three-Mile Creek, it runs past the Hundred-and-Fifty you know, where the robberies were.

II

It runs past the Hundred-and-Fifty clean down to the Mission. It goes down and into the lake, I guess.

They have another water at the Mission that comes from Lac La Hache. That's their own. An early priest took it up — the priest that first settled the Mission. I don't know his name. That was before my time.

They say he recorded the water for a hundred years, yes. He must have been looking forward.

So when somebody was living in that house beyond the Mission where the old road used to be, and they wanted to take the water, they couldn't do nothing.

The Father had the papers — the water rights — for a hundred years and better, I guess. He was looking forward, not back.

He was a college-educated man, they say.

So I was telling Sammy not to forget what you learn.

III

My husband was half Indian. He had a Welsh father, yes. But he went to school at the Mission. Things didn't pan out, so the Father let him go. He went back to Comer's Ranch where he worked. He worked for his schooling there. He went to school at the Hundred-and-Fifty. He had to work to get it. But he wasn't highly educated. No diplomas. No nothing! I didn't get no diplomas either. No nothing!

22

IV

When I came from school I didn't like the way things were. I didn't like what I saw among my people.

So I read. I had books. I had newspapers My father used to buy the paper — the *Sun* or the *Province*. Yes, he used to get it and make us read. He used to make us read.

He used to make us not to forget what we had learned. He used to make us not to forget how to figure — to figure out his grain when he sells them.

V

I was never very good at figuring. I never got a diploma or anything.

My husband used to say, "How much hay is on that load, Augusta?" And I never could say "A ton, or half-a-ton, or two ton."

My back used to say, "It's a lot of hay, Augusta!", but my head couldn't tell us how much.

That's why it's good not to forget what you have learned.

Premature

I had four children, two boys and two girls.
My daughters were babies when they died.
Yes, small babies.

My daughters were born before their time.
They say a child born at six months will live,
But not at eight!

That's what they claim, and so they died.
No doctor, no help. If your child was sick
It had to die.

That's the way it was in those days.

Doctor's Book

I bought a doctor's book from Eatons.
It was down at Regina then.
It cost me three dollars, yes.

But I read that book from end to end.
I learned it by heart.
At night in my kitchen by candlelight.

It was this thick and it had pictures
About everything — mother, baby, boils, breaks,
Yes, I learned it by heart.

I said, "I'm not scared to help them."
No doctors, nobody; so I learned that book
And I helped them.

At Birth

I used to help at times of birth, yes,
I used to help all the women around here.
I learned it from my book, my blue doctor's book.
I used to read it all the time.

I made up my mind that if she needs help,
I will help her. I'm not scared.
You've got to be awfully quick. There's two lives there.
The baby and the mother.

Yes, two lives, and what you got to do it with
Those days? You've got to be quick
To cut the cord, keep the bed clean, take out
The afterbirth, discard it, burn it.

Yes, you've got to be quick, fix the baby,
Tie its navel so it will not bleed
To death — cut it about that long.
When it heals there's nothing left, you know.

Then you bandage the mother, pin her up,
Keep her clean, keep her in bed ten days.
The doctor told us this — but if I leave,
I guess she got up.

I never had to spank a baby
To make him cry — they always cried.
They were always alive and healthy.
Yes, mother and baby, alive and healthy.

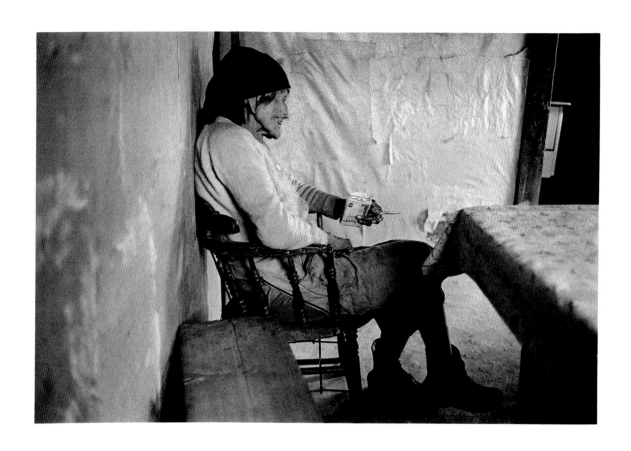

Smallpox

I

It must have been about 1860, that smallpox time. My grandmother told me. She lived through it. Not many did.

She said that lots of Indians lived on this high bench and that's where they are all buried. They died like flies, yes.

And for years after, a flag used to wave above the gravcyard, but that's gone now. But no one goes near it anyhow. No one wants to go near it.

How they got it she says was from a man on foot coming through the country. A white man. A miner, maybe, in those days.

He camped near the Indians and they gave him food and were good to him. And I guess he thanked them by giving them this nice blanket — a Hudson's Bay blanket, my grandmother says.

Well, that man didn't have smallpox — no, he didn't have it. But they figured out later that he must have carried it with him in that blanket.

They all got it anyway after he left. It cleaned them out.

II

Well, my grandmother's young brother got this smallpox. They were young in those days. She didn't get it because she stayed away from the others. She was living in an underground house.

Her brother called to her. "Make a fire out here for me," he called.

My grandmother tells him to "come in".

"I told you not to go over there," she tells him. "I told you to stay away!"

Well, I guess he was dying, see, and it wasn't long till he died.

And my granny — I guess she had one of these ladders, you know, to get out of her house, made out of a tree, a limb left on this side and a limb left on that side right up for the feet to go on — well, my granny says she carried him out, yes, over her shoulder and she buried him.

She had quite an effort you know, But I guess she was strong in those days.

Anyhow, she lived and they died.

III

Then the 'flu came, yes. Years after, the 'flu came. It was when the soldier boys were coming home. My grandmother was old then, old and weak, I guess. It took her, yes.

She lived through the smallpox, but not the 'flu. That 'flu finished her.

I was sick with the 'flu. I couldn't get up and help nobody! I couldn't help granny.

I raised up in bed after they told me and I looked out the window. I saw my granny's coffin. It was bouncing around in the back of the rig. They were hauling her down to the graveyard to bury her. About a mile down the hill.

I couldn't go. But I saw her go. I saw my granny go.

The Story of the Sturgeon

There was this one time I saw a sturgeon caught in the Fraser River. It was where Deep Creek empties into the river near Hargreaves Ranch. Yes, there is this big eddy there — deep too.

Deep Creek is this creek where I'm standing talking to you one day.

Well, this man, Captain Charlie — that one who caught the sturgeon — he must have got Billy Lyon to make him two hooks. They were joined together like this, back-to-back. Oh, they were big hooks, huge hooks. Made like a fish hook, exactly the same as a fish hook, but large!

Well, this old man, Captain Charlie, he was a pure Indian from Lillooet and he married a Soda Creek woman, I guess; is where he lived anyhow. Well, he must have known the sturgeon lived there in that eddy. He must have watched.

He got ready to catch the sturgeon, yes, Captain Charlie got ready. You would have to get ready to catch a sturgeon. He's not a little fish!

In my language — in Shuswap — the sturgeon and the whale are the same thing. It is just called by one name — *wholt*! It means the whale and the sturgeon. *Wholt* — just that. I can't tell you how to spell it — that Shuswap, that's hard!

I saw this sturgeon. Oh, it was nine feet at least. It was a monster, yes, I saw that one.

It was before I was married. I was single, staying down there with my father and mother. My father was going to water the horses. You see, we had a wagon and a team, and those horses would not drink river water. They wanted fresh water that comes from Deep Creek. So we had to take them down there.

And that's when we found out a sturgeon had been caught.

We passed him, Captain Charlie, (he was riding horseback), and he said he had caught a sturgeon. He said he had to go to his house for something. He said, "I'll be back pretty soon." I guess he went for his son.

Well, we stayed around to help. He and his wife had a camp there at the mouth of Deep Creek by the big eddy. It was where they had the hook fixed and I guess they wouldn't leave that.

Well, this sturgeon, it had come up out of the eddy and it had taken the bait — a whole salmon — and it was hooked, and from the hooks, to keep the sturgeon from smelling human beings, they had a braided willow for several feet. They had peeled a willow and braided it — spring's the only time you can peel that willow. It's white when you peel it. When spring is here, it just comes right off, you know, the sap is run. It's their rope in the early days, long ago.

Well, it's what the old man had on these two hooks. It was braided about that big, like my wrist, and it was tied from the hooks to the main rope — the bought rope.

Well, Captain Charlie had all this coiled and staked by the river — staked with a long stick. So, if the sturgeon took the hook, the stick was missing, understand? That stick that was standing by the shore with the coiled rope around it, then if it wasn't there, well the sturgeon had the hook. The rest of the rope went up to a big tree, way up on shore, way up there, the rope did. Oh, it was a long rope, about from here to the gate — about two hundred feet? A long rope.

And the sturgeon bit the hooks, yes — swallowed them and it was right down here in the stomach. It was baited with a whole fresh salmon. That sturgeon had a big mouth. The head stood that high, I guess, as high as my table. Oh, it was a big thing that one I saw.

It swallowed the hook, and it was hooked against its insides in the rib part. You couldn't pull that hook out.

The sturgeon went as far as the rope would let it go. It was fighting the rope when we got there. It wasn't splashing the water. It was just going this way and that way.

And we started pulling on this rope. Captain Charlie, my father, we all held on and pulled at the same time. There were three of us close to the river and the grandson of this old man who had the hooks in, he was riding a horse and hanging on the rope and pulling with that horse.

It took us quite a while to pull this thing out. It fought. It was strong too, my God! It jerked this way and it jerked that way. It kept doing that and we kept pulling. When we thought it would start back this way, we'd pull again. Oh, we had to work hard to help to get it.

The horse was over there holding tight on that long rope. No one shouted. Everyone kept quiet. Didn't want to scare the sturgeon any more than he was. We'd let it have rope, you know, but we stood there on the shore to take it up again. It kept fighting the hook this way and that way.

Finally it came toward the shore, little by little — getting tired, I guess. And I guess this hook was hurting too. It must have. Yes, it must have hurt.

So finally, we landed it.

The old lady, Mrs. Captain Charlie, made lots of leaves, stripped the trees of leaves and spread them on the ground, spread them 'way out. Well, it was a big thing, you know.

34

So we finally landed it. And we put that sturgeon on top of the leaves to keep it clean. It died. It died from no water. Still he hammered it with an axe, the single-blade axe. Not the double-bitted, but the single-blade. Captain Charlie did this, yes. And he hit it three or four times to be sure it died. Well, when it kept still, we knew it was dead.

Then we flopped it on its back. We all helped. My father helped and my cousin helped — (she's dead, my father's dead, and all those fellows are dead; I'm the only one that's alive) — well, they flopped it onto its back and then they opened it up.

Yes, they opened it up and it had this — I can't tell you what they called it — it's a white thing. It looks like grease, you know, grease that comes from the butcher's, but it looked soft. It was white and it was big! And the way nature made it, it was full of little purple eggs — just full, anyway you turned the thing, it was just full. Where you cut it, it was just full of it.

I didn't cut it. It wasn't ours to cut. It was Captain Charlie's. We were just looking on — what happened and what it looks like.

Anyway, the old lady took it away. She put it on something clean. She said she was going to look at it to see what she would do with it. I don't know what she did with it, but it must have been useful.

But when we were looking at this sturgeon's stomach, we saw it had three more dead salmon inside. Yes, beside the one it swallowed for bait. That made four!

But I'll tell you, while he was butchering this fish here, while Captain Charlie was butchering this fish, we could hear the water in the eddy start to rumble and it started to roll — there in the eddy where he caught this fish. He told us to keep quiet. So we all stood up, we all stood up and we were looking to see what would come up from the river.

We were all scared too when it kept on rumbling and rumbling — loud, good and loud. And then we saw it! It was another sturgeon. And it brought its whole body out of the water like this, shooting water through its nostrils, like a whale. And the water curled up like this and fell back into the river and the sturgeon came up again and again.

And we were scared, yes. We were scared.

And soon it was quiet again. The eddy was quiet and still.

Old Captain Charlie, he says, "He's going away now." That's what he told us. He says, "He misses his mate and now he is going away. He has said goodbye."

I guess they had been living there in the eddy, those two sturgeon, right there in the big eddy where the river runs deep.

My Grandfather Spoke French

My grandfather, he spoke good French.
Father Thomas too spoke good French.

One day I heard them laughing and talking.
They were having a joke.

We asked Grandpa later,
"What were you telling the Father?"

"Oh, nothing much," he told us —
But he wouldn't tell.

He wouldn't tell what was their joke,
Walking down the road to the church.

My Paternal Grandfather
and My Maternal Grandfather

My father was a northern Indian; he was born up here.
But my grandfather, he came from Red River someplace —
and he could speak French-Canadian language; but my father,
he didn't know French —
only my grandfather.

My grandmother, my grandfather's wife, died up this way,
that is, my father's mother died up this way.
Him and his brother were left alone, yes,
and his sister, his small sister — a little girl —
they were left alone.

Well, they all grew up, yes,
they all grew up in their own way.

My mother was born in Soda Creek, a chief's daughter, yes,
my maternal grandfather was the chief.
This grandfather was born in Soda Creek
and he was a chief, yes,
he was a chief.

These days they elect their chiefs; Sugar Cane has George Abbey;
Alkali has Irwin Harry, yes, they elect their chiefs;
but in my grandfather's day, his father must have been a chief
and his father must have been a chief
because it was handed down.

It belonged to them in those days.
It was their right —
It was hereditary.

William Longshem was his name. When they had a meeting
down in Ashcroft of all the chiefs,
he had to go, yes,
William Longshem, he had to go.

They didn't have a ceremony when a man became a chief,
anyway, I don't remember a ceremony.
I guess they had their times, yes,
before my time,
I guess they did.

"We had a Priest..."

We had a priest who talked Shuswap.
He was an early, early priest, yes.
He died from appendicitis,
or old age, or something.
Anyhow, he died.

Since 1931

I was still a young woman when my husband died,
since 1931, quite a while ago,
I've been all alone, struggling,
yes, struggling.

I've watched the years go by since he's been gone,
the seasons; the hunting seasons
and the fishing seasons, struggling
since he's been gone.

But since my pension come on you know
I make out alright.
I have to look after it though.
Things are so high.

Especially meat and eggs, they are high and going up.
It's a dollar-and-a-half
for a little chunk like that of meat
Huh? — not very big!

Sometimes we get wild meat when my son kills them
for his family.
I used to get a little.
We share it around.

It's a long time since 1931.

The Captive Girl

It is a long time ago, but they used to steal women then. Yes, I'll tell you about it. I'll tell you about one woman who was taken. My grandmother told me this and it's true.

There were three women. Well, two women and one of them had a daughter with her. Well, the daughter, I guess, she was about thirteen. In those days, they got married early. She was married or about to get married, so I guess she was a woman, really.

They went out to pick saskatoons. There were no more berries down Soda Creek, so they went 'way out.

Going up this hill, they saw some trees tied up together like this, you know, and this woman who didn't have a daughter with her, she got afraid.

She said, "Let's go back. This don't look right."

But this other woman said, "Oh, I guess some kids came along and tied the trees like that."

Anyhow, the first woman I guess decided to stay on, even though she didn't feel just so. But they had lunch with them and they had reached good saskatoon country just this side of Big Lake. That's quite a ways, you know. But this woman I guess she kept thinking those trees tied up was a warning.

Anyhow, they picked berries and they had lunch and sometime later, they went to bed under a tree.

They didn't know this man was watching them. They didn't know there were other men near by. I guess they were coming to steal some women, coming from a long distant country. Some said Cree and some said *sicom* — that's my language — it means far-off people. And Cree is supposed to be in Alberta. But which of those I don't know.

But anyhow, there was one man there. He didn't want to hurt these women, so that night, I guess when the other men had gone to sleep, he got up and went to where these women were sleeping. He poked one of them on her forehead...with a stick. She woke up and she looked up and there was a man making signs to her, telling her not to talk and to go home. That was no place here for them.

Well, she understood it, this woman without a daughter. And the next morning, she wanted to come home to Soda Creek. Well, this other woman was determined to pick berries and of course her daughter would stay with her.

Well, that's when these men took her daughter. The other woman, the smart one, she ran off. She didn't show herself. She could hear this girl screaming and the old lady, too. The old lady hung on to her daughter, and they told her to let go. But she wouldn't. So they killed her and took the girl. They didn't care for nobody, you know.

Anyhow, they took the girl. She wasn't really a girl, but they thought she was single. They didn't know she was married or about to be. So they took her a long way back to their country and they put her with a woman of their own tribe. This woman had her own hut or tent — it was too early for tents — it must have been a hut of some sort and she had to guard and look after this girl.

Well anyhow, soon they found out she was to be a mother. Well this let them out, see? They hadn't counted on this. But they put her there and this woman was good to her. Yes, nice to her. I guess their language was different, is all.

In the meantime, the woman who was smart enough to run away told the people at Soda Creek what had happened. They went looking for the girl. But they never found her. They just found where she had been made to dance and had lost the feathers out of her headband. And I guess they found the mother, killed.

So the girl stayed with this woman in the hut, and she stayed there and stayed there till her child was born. And when they found out it was a boy, they took it away and threw it in the river.

"If this boy grows up, he might kill us all," they said. "Might as well kill it and throw it away. If it was a girl, we would have kept it. It would have done us no harm." That is what they were saying to this woman. So they took it.

It broke the girl's heart, you know, to see her baby taken away and thrown in the water.

Anyway, I guess the woman in the hut pitied the girl. She made up her mind to help her escape. She started making mocassins for her to wear and dried food to carry with her and then she told the girl to go.

So she took off.

She came to a river that she had to cross and there about the center was a log jam — logs all piled up from when the river starts to get higher. Well, she made it to the log jam, how I don't know. Maybe by swimming. And then she heard dogs barking and men shouting. They were looking for her. They found out she had escaped. But she hid in the log pile.

The dogs came down and smelled her tracks where they had gone into the water. And the men came running behind carrying long sticks with sharp points on and they were trying to find her. But they couldn't see her. But she was looking at them; looking at them.

Well finally they gave up and went home. She waited and waited until there was no more noise and then she came out. She was wet and her mocassins and her lunch were all gone. She had sunk down you know on that log pile and was all wet.

She rested awhile, I guess and then she took off, went on her way. She knew what she had to do. She knew where she had to go.

So she kept a-coming, kept a-coming. She was hungry, you know. She saw some wild chickens. She stoned them. Killed them. She skinned them off, peeled them off and hung them over her shoulders to dry while she was walking. Only way she could eat them, you know, was dried. She didn't have no matches. She had nothing.

When they were kind of dry, she would eat them. It was her lunch, you know.

She kept a-coming and a-coming until she got 'way up into this big valley and she knew she was close to home. She kept a-coming until she landed at Soda Creek, right down here.

Her people were all across the river. They used to live across the river then. And I guess she was pretty weak by this time, but she tried, and she raised her arms and waved to them. And they saw her, yes, they saw her wave.

She laid down then, all sore, all hungry and so weak that she laid down. She laid down to wait.

They came across in canoes and they had blankets — buckskin blankets — there were no blankets as we know them, They loaded her into the canoe and took her home. They looked after her until she got better. They give her lots of fish soup, I quess. It would make her strong again.

And she lived. How long she lived after that, it doesn't say, but she lived in spite of everything.

My grandmother told me this. It's true.

Death of a Son

Yes, Joe died, my oldest son, he died.

He got hurt one morning and he died
at eight o'clock that night same day.
He got hurt just over there where our fence
follows the old highway.

He was work for Hargreave's Ranch that time.
He tied his lunch on the saddle and got up on this horse
and went look for cattle down toward Deep Creek, yes.
Cattle used to roam all over the country, you know.

But he didn't make it, no, he didn't make it.

This horse he had it was still quite wild.
It didn't fully understand the bridle yet.
If you pull it too hard, it used to fall back.
If you spurred it, it would straighten out.

But he didn't have spurs on, no, he didn't have spurs.

I was packing water from the spring 'way down the hill.
I heard someone yell; I heard him calling me.
I dropped my buckets and I ran, my God!
I ran through high grass and bush; I fell, I ran and I fell again.

I found him lying there in the grass, yes, I found him.

I don't know just what really happened.
I think this wild horse wanted to cross the fence
to our other horses and he bolted or bucked
or jumped and fell — but I don't know really what happened.

Except Joe lay there with a hole in his head, yes, in his head.

Is what killed him, I guess. His lunch was smashed.
George threw it away and we took him down to hospital
at the Lake, but they couldn't do nothing.
He died at eight o'clock that night same day.

When I carry water from the spring sometimes
I hear him calling from over there. But he's not there, no.

I buried him at the Mission. I buried my son at the Mission.

Dickie

I raised lots of children beside my own.
I raised Mabel and Lucille and Lucille's children.
Yes, I raised lots of children —
I don't know all who I raised.
There was Dickie —

I guess somebody reported it to the Welfare
and this man and woman came.
Oh, I don't know what was the matter, no.
He says, "Are you Mrs. Augusta Evans?"
I said, "Yes."

I was out there working making wood
and cleaning the woodshed when they came.
I didn't expect anybody to be coming.
They had a nice car. I didn't know
What was what.

"We'd like to speak to you, Mrs. Evans
about something that's very important
you might like to know."
"Well," I says, "come in. Sure I like to hear
What's what. I like to know
What's what."

They came in.
They told me about Dickie.

I said, "Sure, bring him here, bring him out
Don't let the poor child lie around the streets."
They brought Dickie out the next day.
He was a nice little chap. He liked to play.

He was so small —
He's about that big now!

Sammy

Sammy is different.
He was always kind of quiet, yes.
He's a big tall man now.

I used to work hard for Sammy.
I used to go down to work
down town all day, yes,
down Soda Creek.

Before daylight I used to take the trail
and go down Soda Creek.
I'd leave Sammy with my brother,
fix all his bottles, lots of bottles.
He took two in an afternoon
and my brother would babysit.

I would cook supper down there
for a big family in Soda Creek.
I wouldn't eat. I would come right up
sometimes in dark, sometimes snow;
do what I had to do for Sammy
to raise him.

He's a big tall man now.

Places I've Worked

I

It was a big house where I cooked and they had a little bathroom, tiny, just big enough for their bath and they had this water running in. Oh, it was nice to work toward the end you know with water running in.

I like it although it was hard work and I was paid forty-five dollars a month, yes. She told me I was well worth over a hundred as far as was go for cooks — but she me, I can't afford it.

She had a big family, yes.

They're all grown up and gone.

II

I don't remember what year that house burned down where I cooked. I was here in my own home. They told me that Doug Houston's house burned down.

They had a chimney. I didn't like the chimney, but what could you do? There were no bricks.

They all left it, you know, they all got out the day the house burned twice for the second time.

Yes, not once, but twice!

The One They Took

They took one on me, the Welfare did.
They put him out at Horsefly.
You see, this one I had was a likeable little fellow,
but he started taking fits.

Well, that woman came for him.
In a way I was kind of sorry
and I was kind of mad at that woman too.
I hated her. I told her,
"What makes you so important now?
Why now to be so important?
The minute I raise him
you come taking him away!"

I didn't want him to go.
But I guess she had orders from people.
You know how everything goes
in these government offices.

I guess I loved him,
that little fellow.

The Woman Who Was Prisoner of the Bear
(Children's Story)

This woman was 'way out in the bush with her parents. Why, it doesn't say. But these people, they used to look for food like anyone else out there.

I guess they were hunting or looking for berries.

Well anyway, they were out there. It got dark and they made a camp. But this other woman — the mother — she didn't like to stay out there. She was scared.

But the young woman, she wasn't scared. I guess she didn't care. So she stayed. She watched her father take her mother home. She watched them leave. But she stayed to go on hunting the next day or picking berries.

Well, she stayed out there and sometime before morning, a bear captured this woman, wherever it was. The bear took her to his den and made her stay there.

She was scared, you know. Well, you couldn't blame her. She had no gun, no nothing. Maybe a small snare was all she had to hunt with. Nothing to speak of.

Well, she stayed in this bear den for a long time. He kept her there. What kind of food the bear gave her, it doesn't say. Berries and roots, I guess. Anyhow she stayed in this bear den where she could eat, where she could sleep.

As time went by, she started to wish for her three brothers. She started to miss them. I guess she wondered why they hadn't come looking for her.

The bear used to lie across the front of the den.

One day she was real homesick. She was wishing for her oldest brother. She was wishing he would come for her and take her home.

The bear said, "You don't have to wish for that oldest brother of yours. He's married and he doesn't give a darn about you. What would he want with you anyway? You don't have to think about him."

So she was sad and she lay there and thought about her second brother. She was wishing he would come for her and take her home.

The bear said, "Oh, you don't have to think about that second brother. He's no good. He likes to be with the girls all the time. You know how it is." He says, "You don't have to think about him. It's no use. He doesn't need you. He's no good."

The young woman was very sad — and getting desperate too I guess. She thought about her youngest brother and she remembered he wasn't very old, nor very big, nor very strong. But she wished for him anyway. She was wishing he would come for her and take her home.

Well, this youngest brother, he was single. And even though he wasn't very old, nor very big, nor even very strong, he wasn't crazy about the girls. He wasn't

interested in anybody but himself yet. He like being alone. But he missed his sister, yes. I guess he sort of loved this sister.

And when the young woman wished for her youngest brother, the bear never moved. He couldn't think of anything bad to say about the youngest brother. He tried, but he couldn't. And as long as he couldn't think of anything bad to say, I guess she kept on wishing. It got through to the youngest brother. Yes, it got through.

So he came and he saved his sister from this bear.

He killed the bear and he took the skin and gave it to his sister. Even though he wasn't very old, nor very big, nor very strong, he did this.

His sister wore the bearskin every day of her life, yes, until she died.

The Year the Salmon Run was Poor

One year the salmon run was poor, yes. They had to go down to Ashcroft that year to fish in the Thompson. My grandparents used to tell me that year they used to walk from all over, Quesnel, Alexandria, Soda Creek, all over, and they had to go down to make fish down at Ashcroft.

I don't remember myself. You see, I was at school at the Mission as a small child about four until I was fifteen when I was discharged. But my grandparents used to tell me all these things.

I don't know why they didn't run, those salmon, but they didn't. There must have been something or other.

I don't know what year it might have been, 1892, or maybe worse than that. Maybe later than that, too, because there was no salmon shortage since I grow up. I can remember my parents leaving me with my grandmother when they went fishing.

It might have been a big slide in the river — it might have been, too, but who knows?

They fished it, you know, the Thompson River. The fish in the Thompson's different from our salmon, yes, a little different. There's the humpback and it's fat. Well, the fish they catch here is not like that. No, it's nice.

They packed it on their backs, two or three packs at a time. They had no horses, no wagons, no nothing. Just a trail. They had to pack it on their backs or go hungry or starve. That winter was nearly here in this country.

They took a trail through Canoe Creek, a shortcut, that year the salmon didn't run.

It's Easy To Make A Net

Yes, it's easy! It's easy to make a net.

It's made from a bush that grows so high;
We call it *shpetsup* meaning cotton.
They take it out of the ground and they dry it.

You have to dry it before you fix it.

They put on gloves to handle it
And they scrape it like this — scrape
Till all the cover is off and leaves the cotton itself.

Yes, it's white and then they fix it up.

They make a string out of it like this, see,
They make a string by twisting it until it gets to be quite a ball.

Then it's ready to make the net.

They start at the bottom *tahajehp* they say,
Tied at the bottom and then they go
Around and around, working two boards, sliding and tying

Until you go clean around, yes.

Many times around until it is this long.
A good net has to be long because it shrinks.
A good net lasts the summer all through fall fishing.

They don't use *shpetsup* any more.
They use coarse string bought at Mackenzie's.
But they say the grass is stronger and better.
You can make a net in a day if you're hurrying to make fish.

It's easy to make a net!

You've got to be Quick

A good net has to be good. It's got a wooden hoop and a wooden handle. They dip it down into the river like this. The minute the salmon goes in, you've got to be quick. You've got to do 'that' with your net and get it out of the water as quick as you can.

A salmon you know gets out of a net a lot faster than he gets into it, yes, he'll jump right out if he can. As fast as that! You've got to be quick!

Gill Net

Gill nets used to be good for fishing trout in the lakes. My mother had her own gill net. She would stake it out in the lake, here and here and here. And when she brought it in, it would be full of trout caught around their gills — yes, full of trout. That fishing is outlawed now.

Gill nets cost a lot. My mother's cost a lot. She paid a horse for it.

Tobacco — Thirty-Five Cents a Plug

Tobacco came to the Indian when the whiteman's stores came in.
It was called T.B. Tobacco, if I remember,
And everyone smoked it, yes, everyone;
Men, women, young women and children,
They smoked it in pipes.

And it was strong, oh, awfully strong, this T.B. Tobacco from the store.
They had to do something with it
Or be sick; so they picked the kinnikinick
And they dried the leaves in a slow oven
To mix with the tobacco in the pipes.

When the leaves were dry, they smashed them up into powder.
They cut the plug tobacco with a sharp knife
Into fine, fine slivers and mixed them together
So that men, women and children, yes, children
Could smoke it in their pipes.

That was before cigarettes, you know,
And it was only thirty-five cents a plug.

The Basket

I

And that's how they make a basket —

With saskatoon wood,
Spruce roots
And thin cherry bark.

The saskatoon wood makes it strong.
The spruce roots make the weave.
The cherry bark is design.

The saskatoon,
The spruce
And the choke cherry tree.

II

It's made of birchbark, this one.
We use them for picking berries.
They're good for berry baskets.

First we cut the birchbark from the tree.
Don't just take any kind.
By the feel of it, yes, how thick —
You've got to pick it out.

Don't just cut it anyway.
You cut it toward the sun this way.
An old man told me "cut toward the sun."

See the dark brown bark lines how short they are.
Is good. The long lines tear.
The short are strong, just as God made them.

Don't just sew with anything.
Use the spruce root where it strings out
Just below the ground.

Take it up with gloves
and peel them and split them —
It's easy when the sap is running.

And make it strong with saskatoon wood
Bent around the brim,
And put a handle on of buckskin.

And there you have a berry basket —
A birchbark berry basket,
Layer on layer, just as God made it.

Mend a Basket

This basket had a buckskin handle.
While Sammy was picking raspberries, it broke.
When he brought it home,
He put a wire handle on it.
He said, "That won't break now, Granny."
I said, "No, that will be good."

Baby Basket

Baby baskets are made different these days — not so good, no, not so good.

In those days we made a frame first of saskatoon branches. They are strong. They make a good frame. Then there are two ways to go:

You can put a covering of birchbark on the frame and sew it tight. Or you can put the saskatoon branches close together and cover it with buckskin, untanned buckskin, so it won't go soft. Yes, either way.

You've got to decide for yourself which way is best. If you use the birchbark you've got to line it. I lined my basket first with cloth all over. Birchbark sweats, you see. Birchbark is tight and won't let out the air. And you've got to keep it dry and clean.

Or you use buckskin — is a strong basket, that buckskin! You don't tan it, no. Just take off the hair and clean the blood out and then you've got to be quick and sew it before it gets dry while the hide is still green. Yes, is a strong basket.

Then inside for the baby — yes, inside you put in the bottom with dried wild hay; they used to cut it and dry it and store it. And you put that hay in the bottom. It has to be clean and dry. I used feathers, yes, for my children I used feathers. And they all have a juniper hoop across the basket near the head to hold the blankets off the baby when he's sleeping. And he's laced in tight and cosy with buckskin thong.

They don't put a spout in no more — but they used to, yes. They used to make a tube of birchbark and sew it and stick it out the botton end. The urine used to go out this way. But as we grew and got civilized, we didn't do this anymore. We did away with the spout.

I don't know about this getting civilized. In those days it's birchbark or buckskin, dry hay or feathers. Now it's cardboard and gingham and no spout for the urine. Our baby basket, our *eklan-day-lah*, it's not so good now, not so good.

The Powder Rock

They say you have to cross the Okanagan Lake
a part of it.
It's a big lake as far as you can see
and the Indians had to cross it yes,
to reach their powder rock.

They used to cross this lake to the camping place
by using a canoe;
birchbark canoes made by their own hands
out of birchbark and strong enough
to cross this big lake.

They'd do their packing what they had to eat,
packing their blankets,
men, women and children, and camp there;
they'd hunt deer, what kind I couldn't say,
down below the powder rock.

This old lady was telling me how high
was the powder rock,
high above their camp and red in the sunset,
red in the sunrise, too, so she said,
and hard to reach.

Some people thought the Indians used rust
to paint themselves,
but it was the powder rock.

If it still stands today I don't know
nothing about it.
The old people knew where it was, I guess.
But this generation won't ever know, I guess.
They don't give a darn.

But they use to paint themselves bright red,
used to smash it up,
dilute it and paint themselves for war,
for celebrations, for what all nobody knows;
to this day, nobody cares.

And they would put feathers in their hair.
This Chief told me
his feathers were white, belonged to an eagle
or some big bird like that, and his face and hands
would be painted bright red.

Some people still say it was rust that we used,
but it was the powder rock.

Whoosham

They call it Indian icecream, that stuff!
Whoosham, whoosham, made from the soapallalie bush.
Made from little red berries.

I boil them without sugar, without sugar.
I put it in a sack and strain it.
The pure juice you get, yes, the pure juice
And you beat it up with sugar.

But you've got to watch, yes.
Everything must be clean — no grease
Or you won't have good luck.
You won't have *whoosham!*

Travel by Winter

I never saw winters like those used to be —
Snow and north winds and cold, yes, cold!

We used to have these bricks, George did,
And he would put them in the oven to get hot.

When they got real hot, George used to put his coat on
And put them in the bottom of the sleigh.

He put gravel in the bottom of the sleigh first
So the bricks wouldn't burn right through the wood.

Oh, I'll say they were real hot!
George used to do this for us when we've been travelling.

And we would travel a long way, yes,
A long way in snow and north winds and cold.

Changes

Marriage changes, you know — always changing.

They say Dunlevy had an Indian wife,
But that was before my time.
When I knew him, he had a white wife
Who married a doctor when he died.

Oh, it was hard on Indian wives, I guess,
But they always managed
To raise their children
Even if their husbands finished with them.

Of course, it isn't right in our civilized days.
In those days they didn't care —
Didn't really marry!
In very early days you couldn't do that.

You were married and your husband kept you
Until he died. And you —
You stayed with him until he died
And that was that.

But it's different now.
There's divorces and parting
And go this way, and go that way —
Always changing.

The Big Tree and the Little Tree

(Children's Story, modernized — a recent version)

There were two trees growing up there in the woods, yes. One was a big tree and the other was small. Well, the big tree grew here and the other tree grew there, you see. They were fir trees — evergreens.

    The big tree used to talk to the little tree all the time.

    "Well," the big tree says, "you're too small. I'm a big tree, but you're too small." He says, "I don't want you to grow near me."

    But what could he do about that? The little tree was there to stay.

    The big tree kept on talking to the other one.

    "I feed the squirrels, but you don't. You're too small yet. But I feed lots of squirrels. I feed them from my tree."

    You see, that was the tree himself that was speaking.

    "And now I have lots of friends among the squirrels. They come and they eat what I feed, but you have nothing. Someday you might be like me, but it will be years and years before you are as big as me, before you will be feeding the squirrels.

    "And the squirrels like me. They come up here and they sleep up here. And birds build their nest up here and live here all summer and raise their families. And people take my branches and make beds when they are out hunting or berry picking. The squirrels like me; they all like me.

    "Later on," he says, "you might grow up to be a big tree and then you might be of some good, but right now," he says, "you're small and useless and nobody seems to care for you. Later on you might be like me. You might be somebody."

    Well, the little tree got the idea from all this that in order to be somebody, he would have to be of some use And as you know, it takes a little tree a long time to grow to be big and useful. So for many years, he had to listen to the big tree telling him how useless he was.

    But he finally did grow up, you know. He grew up and started to feed the squirrels his fine, fat cones. And birds started to nest in his branches and they liked it there. And people would take his branches to make beds and they said they were the softest beds they had ever had. And the little tree was very happy for himself.

    But it made him sad to see the other tree, which had been the big tree at one time, getting older and dying slowly from the top down. Yes, he felt sad for the old tree. He was taller than the old tree by now and he felt sad for him.

    And then there came a time when people came with sacks and they stooped down under the younger tree and picked up all his fallen cones. And they were excited

about his cones. He heard them say they were the best in the whole country and they would be sent far, far away to start a whole new forest in another country.

This made the young tree feel very important.

"Yes," said the older tree, "you have become important. At last you have become useful." And the old tree was very sad. "The squirrels don't come to eat my old cones anymore. They go to you. The birds don't nest on my branches anymore. They're old and brittle and might break. People don't use them for beds anymore. They wouldn't be able to sleep on them. They all go to you. They all love you."

But instead of laughing at the old tree, the young tree looked down at him.

"You mustn't cry," he said. "You have been a good and useful tree. Without you, I wouldn't be here. I am one of your children. I am part of you. My cones are your cones. My branches are your branches. When I was small, you spread your branches over me so the snow wouldn't break me down. You got scorched when the forest fire went by, but you protected me. You scared away the deer when it wanted to nibble my tender shoots. You took care of me and that is why I have grown to be so tall. You have been the most useful tree in the forest.

"Together, our cones will start a new forest in a far away land. It will be the finest forest in the world."

You see, the most important thing the young tree ever did was not feeding the squirrels or nesting the birds or bedding the people or growing the best cones. The most important thing was making the old tree happy in his old age.

They were both happy ever since.

"It Never Should Have Happened"

Those little barrels of whisky made all that trouble, yes.
They weren't big — you could pack one yourself —
Or any woman could pack it.
But it made trouble.

You see, this pack train was coming along Springhouse trail —
Lots of packhorses loaded with heavy freight,
Headed for Barkerville, I guess,
And lots of whisky.

It never should have happened, you know.
They shouldn't have done it.

Well anyhow, here's all these Indian tribes camping,
Having a *sputlum* near Springhouse.
I don't how how you say *sputlum*
In English language.

It means to stay and come — a gathering place
For all those who speak Shuswap, yes.
And they got into that whisky.
I don't know who was to blame.

Maybe the Indians demanded it, maybe it was sold them;
But it shouldn't have happened.

Well, the drivers knew they had to show up in Barkerville
With some of the whisky if not all;
But the watchman that night,
He was murdered.

Yes, they killed him and nearly everyone got drunk
And the partner, he headed for town,
And then the police came.
They called them soldiers those days.

They arrested the killers, yes, and put them to jail
And they waited in there for Judge Begbie.
When he came that term and heard the charge,
He said they could hang!

Well, it never should have happened, you know.

Oh, it was a big affair for this country, that hanging —
Two or three of them on the gallows
At the old Comer Ranch
And everybody come to watch.

Well, this is what they want, for everyone to hear
Judge Begbie tell them what's what
About the law in Cariboo
So it shouldn't happen again.

My mother-in-law told me she heard him, she was there.
He said there would be no more killing,
No Indian would kill a white man,
Or a white man an Indian.

Or a Chinaman, or each other, or a man a woman —
Oh, I guess he had a lot of explaining to do;
Nobody understood English much those days.
No Indians understood.

My mother-in-law, she didn't understand at first.
You see, a white man came to her house
With a bundle under his arm.
"Will you sew for me?" he says.

It meant some money, I guess, and it's always good!
"Yes," she said, "I sew for you."
He gave her a roll of black yard goods
To make three pillowcases.

"Do you know what you have made?" he asked her
When he came back for them.
"If you don't, you go to Comer Ranch tomorrow
And find out."

And that's where she saw the black 'pillowcases' again —
At Comer Ranch, on the gallows.

It never should have happened, you know.
They shouldn't have done it.

JEAN E. SPEARE was born into a pioneer British Columbia family and was raised on a Cariboo ranch. She spent a large part of her life in Barkerville, and her writing about the Cariboo has appeared in many newspapers in British Columbia.

At the time *The Days of Augusta* was written, Jean and her husband lived in Williams Lake. Now both retired, they live in Quesnel, B.C., where their interests centre on promoting hiking trails in the Barkerville country.

ROBERT KEZIERE is a Vancouver photographer. He took the magnificent, intimate photographs in this book over the better part of two weeks, photographing Augusta Tappage in the cabin that each year became her summer home.

Robert Keziere's photographs have been exhibited in Canada, the United States and Europe and are in a number of public and private collections, including the Canada Council Art Bank and the Canadian Museum of Contemporary Photography.